SHIP OF DREAMS

DEAN MORRISSEY

HARRY N. ABRAMS, INC., PUBLISHERS
IN ASSOCIATION WITH MILL POND PRESS, INC.
A SCHOLASTIC SCHOOL MARKET EDITION

For Kate and Ian, the stars above us.

Joey's friend Henry claimed that he had seen the Sandman the night before. Henry sometimes made up stories.

Joey was wide awake when he climbed into bed that night. He had made up his mind to stay awake and try to catch a glimpse of the Sandman.

"What does he look like? How big is he?" Joey had asked Henry. "Does he fly? Did you see him sprinkle the sleeping sand? Were you scared?" Joey had a hundred questions.

"Well," Henry had replied, "it was sort of dark so I couldn't see very well, but I'll tell you this, he was there. And then he was gone, in the blink of an eye."

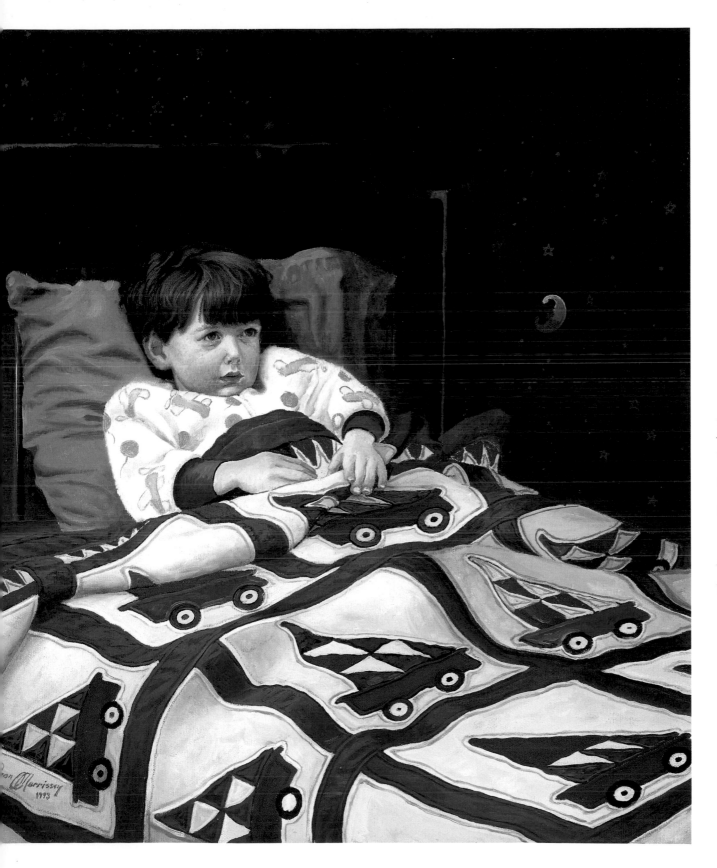

Joey lay in bed
waiting
and watching
and listening.

After a while he began
to grow sleepy.

To keep from falling asleep Joey tried to picture the Sandman in his mind.

"I'll bet he wears a robe and slippers and has a long white beard. I wonder how he carries all that sleeping sand around. If I was the Sandman, I'd take the Redd Rocket."

The Redd Rocket was Joey's wagon. He'd been riding in it all afternoon. Around the backyard, up the driveway, and through the garden they'd gone, with adventure at every turn.

Joey wondered how he could make his wagon fly, and what he would need to bring along.

"I'd use a balloon to lift it up into the sky and a sail to catch the wind. I'd load the sleeping sand on board, and, what else?

"Oh, supplies, food and stuff. Let's see . . .
a map, and a box of animal crackers, some string and a chocolate bar, grapes and an apple.

"A compass, an extra chocolate bar, and my baseball cap.
An orange, my blanket and pillow, a chocolate ba . . . ."

Joey's eyes began to close.

A sudden bouncing and banging startled the boy awake. He sat up to find himself sitting in the Redd Rocket and hurtling through the night sky.

Past the town clock tower, over the rooftops and chimneys he flew. Metal wheels rattled, and a cloth sail flapped in the wind. Joey gripped the sides of the wagon in fright.

"Hey! . . . Wait! . . . Stop!!"

Higher and higher the little wagon climbed, away from the village rooftops and into the dark night.

"Maybe I'm just dreaming!" Joey hoped out loud as he hung on for dear life.

But soon the wagon slowed, and his fear gave way to wonder. He looked around to find himself drifting through a heavenly field of golden stars. A crescent moon came into view. A shooting star streaked by in the distance.

"Where am I?" asked Joey as he relaxed his grip and looked around in amazement.

Just then . . . .

BAM!

The wagon ran right
into another crescent
moon and tipped over.
Joey lost his balance and
tumbled out into the sky.

Rolling and tumbling he went . . .
spinning and falling . . .
down and down . . .
And down he fell.

All seemed lost, when suddenly, out of nowhere, something snatched him from his terrifying plunge and held him fast.

Joey's heart was pounding.
        He looked around frantically.

    "Ropes?" he gasped. "I'm in a net!"

    A very large net in fact, and it was floating in midair.

Joey peered out through the ropes.
All about him stars and moons twinkled and bobbed
in the night sky.

Up close the stars were very big, bigger than Joey. A
few of them had numbers on them, but most had
names and fancy designs.

"Where am I?" Joey wondered as he searched the sky
for an answer. "What am I doing here?"

A voice boomed out of the darkness

Just then a voice boomed out of the darkness. "Who's there?"

Joey spun around. He looked out where the voice had come from. There, sailing straight toward him, was a strange ship. It was very big. Sails billowed out and a great balloon rose from the center.

Joey could see an old man pacing back and forth at the rail as the ship drifted closer. He was grumbling to himself, gesturing with his hands.

Right up over the net the ship sailed. Suddenly it stopped.

"I say, who's there?" the man bellowed down.

Joey tried to speak, but nothing came out.

"Very well," said the man. "We'll soon see."

Joey felt a sudden yank as the old man began pulling the net toward the ship.

"Help!" he yelled.

Hand over hand the man hauled in the net. Over the rail came Joey. Ropes, bells, and all he tumbled onto the deck.

Frantically he tried to untangle himself.

The old man leaned over him.

"Shooting stars!" he snapped. "This net is for catching shooting stars, not little boys who drop out of the sky in the middle of the night!"

The old man stared down at Joey.

Joey looked back and tried to speak, "I . . ."

"You know it's lucky I spotted you," the old man interrupted, "you could have been . . ." He adjusted his glasses. "Joey! I should have guessed it was you when I saw that red wagon tumbling through the sky."

He reached down and freed the boy from the net.

He tumbled onto the deck

"Who is this man?" Joey wondered. "How does he know me? I want to go home!"

His eyes darted about. The ship was old and worn looking. It creaked and groaned as it swayed back and forth in the sky.

Joey turned and looked into the open hatchway on the deck. He could see that the ship's hold was filled with sparkling golden sand.

"Sand?" he thought. "Sand? Wait a minute, the beard, the robe . . ." Joey turned and looked up at the old fellow. "You . . . you're the Sandman!"

The man was silent for a moment. Then, bowing slightly, he said, "The one and only."

"I was waiting to see you when all of this happened!" Joey exclaimed. "Wow, it really is you. Just like I imagined. Wait till I tell Henry."

The ship's hold was filled with sparkling golden sand

"I can see you've got a head full of questions, Joey, but right now we've got to make up for lost time," said the Sandman.

He walked to the ship's big wooden wheel and called out, "Alright now, hang on!" He clapped his hands together and gold dust swirled up from the hatch. Joey could feel the ship begin to move as it set out on a sea of stars.

Soon, the sky began to grow light. "What I do, Joey, is to fly just behind the sunset and follow it right around the world," the Sandman explained. "That way I drift into each town at bedtime to get the children off to sleep. Luckily, I'd finished my rounds when you dropped in or my schedule would have been a mess," he said. "Now I've got one more thing to do and then we'll see about getting you home."

A big trunk that's chock full of the most extraordinary things

Joey tried to take in what the Sandman had been saying. "Do you mean you sprinkle sleeping sand on every child in the world?"

"Every child, every night, no exceptions," came the reply.

Joey had so many questions he hardly knew where to begin. But one question came first. "Do you know what happened to the Redd Rocket when I fell? I guess it's gone for good."

"Not to worry, Joey, I caught it in one of my nets. I'll see that you get it back. It's amazing the things I've caught in those shooting star nets over the years. I've made a sort of hobby collecting the stuff. Back home in my windmill I've got a big trunk that's chock full of the most extraordinary things, everything from a polka dot walrus to a one-handed pocket watch. You name it, I've got it."

"Now then," he said, looking out over the bow of the ship, "if my charts are right we should be coming to the spot."

The ship slowed to a stop. Reaching over the side, the old man hoisted up a large golden star that had been hanging from the rail. Across it was the name Kate.

Holding the star out over the side of the ship, the Sandman asked, "Does that look straight, Joey?"

"Yes. I think so."

The Sandman closed his eyes and began to speak:
"Through stardust and comets
and wind and bad weather,
may this star that I hang in the sky
stay forever!"

He pulled his hands away. The star floated in place.

"Wow!" said Joey. "How did you do that?"

"Well, let's just say it takes a lot of practice," said the Sandman.

"But why do you put stars in the sky? Aren't there enough already?"

"Every time a child is born I make a new star and hang it in the sky above the town where they were born. Kate was born down there. This is her star.

"Now off we go, no time to waste if we're going to get you home by morning."

May this star that I hang in the sky stay forever

"Where will you go after you take me home?" Joey asked.

"Across the sea and back to my windmill," the Sandman replied. "I need a few winks of sleep myself. Work starts at sunrise."

"But I thought the Sandman only worked at night."

"That's what a lot of people think. People imagine that I just drift about all night sprinkling a bit of sand here and there. Let me tell you it's hard work," said the Sandman. "Just for instance, where do you think the sleeping sand comes from?"

"Well, I never thought . . ." Joey started.

"I'll tell you where," the Sandman continued. "Every morning I sail into the sky and harvest the shooting stars that I've caught in my nets— along with any stray little boys that I happen to find, of course."

"Then I take the stars back to the windmill and grind them into fine sleeping sand. That's where it comes from."

"What about the new stars? How do you make those?" asked Joey.

The Sandman was delighted that Joey was so interested in his work. He didn't often get a chance to talk to anyone about it.

"Some of the sand I load onto the ship for sleeping, and some I use to make new stars. I melt the sand in the furnace and pour it into a mold. When it cools, a new star is born. And when a new child is born, I engrave their name on it and hang it in the sky."

I melt the sand

in the furnace

Joey looked out at the night sky twinkling with stars and moons as they sailed along. "There are so many stars up here. How do you keep track of them all?"

"With telescopes, charts, and star maps that I keep in the dome of the windmill," the Sandman answered. "I have maps here on board as well, and a log book, too. I write down the names and positions of all the stars on the maps and in the book."

"But some of the stars have numbers," said Joey.

"Those are my navigating stars. At night they help me to find my way around up here. Sort of like street signs and house numbers, if you know what I mean."

Joey nodded.

"Aha!" announced the Sandman. "Off the starboard bow. Star Number 6. That means we're right above your town, Joey. We'll have you home in no time at all."

I write down the
names and positions
of all the stars

Is there a star up here for me?

Joey wasn't quite sure he wanted to go home yet. He was having a fine time, and he didn't want it to end.

He looked down over the side of the ship. He could just make out the rooftops of his town far below as the dawn began to break.

Turning back to the Sandman, he asked, "Is there a star up here for me?" The old man knelt on one knee beside Joey and pointed into the sky. "Right out there."

The boy searched the sky. "Hey, there it is. Right there," he hollered. "It has my name on it and everything!" Then he paused. "How long will it stay up there?"

The Sandman spoke softly. "Through stardust and comets and wind and bad weather, a star that I place in the sky stays forever."

The ship settled like a giant beanbag

The ship settled like a giant beanbag onto the roof of Joey's house in the early light of dawn.

"Here we are, my boy. Safe and sound and right on time."

Joey looked around the ship trying to take it all in so he wouldn't forget this night. Then he looked at the Sandman. "Will I ever see you again?" he asked.

"I'll be by to see you tonight, as always."

"Well, okay," said Joey. "Good-bye for now, and thanks for everything."

Joey paused. "Oh . . . ah, just one more question. How come I'm not sleepy from being on a ship full of sleeping sand?"

The Sandman placed his hand on the boy's shoulder. "Just open your eyes and everything will become clear."

Joey's eyes slowly opened

Joey's eyes slowly opened. He sat up to find himself at home in his bed. Morning light streamed in through the bedroom window. He rubbed his eyes.

"I guess I must have been dreaming," he thought. "I guess there's nothing to tell Henry. But it all seemed so real."

Just then a ray of sun flashed into the corner of the room, lighting up his toybox.

"I knew it!" cried Joey.

There on his toy chest sat the Redd Rocket. It was fully rigged, with a sail, a balloon, and everything. Just like the night before. Just like it was when he'd sailed with the Sandman.

"He said he'd bring it back!

"Henry just won't believe this. He won't believe a word of it."

Joey paused for a minute. A smile came over his face.

"Maybe I won't tell him."

Editor: Robert Morton
Designer: Liz Trovato
Library of Congress Catalog Card Number: 95–105694
ISBN 0–590–60001–X

Published in 1994 by Harry N. Abrams, Incorporated, New York
A Times Mirror Company
in association with Mill Pond Press, Inc.,
Venice, Florida, publisher of
Dean Morrissey's limited edition art prints

Printed and bound in Hong Kong

Index to Artwork